CHOREBOT

ROX'S SECRET CODE

POW!

BROOKLYN, NY

{CREATED BY}
Mara
Lecocq

{WRITTEN BY}
Nathan
Archambault

{ILLUSTRATED BY}
Jessika Von
Innerebner

{TECH LED BY}
Rodolfo
Dengo

Rox pressed 'Enter' and PonyBot raised a fist high into the air. Her latest robot masterpiece was ready to lead the PrinCentaur revolution!

You see, Rox had a superpower.

She could make any toy she imagined come to life.

Rox was a coder. She knew how to write instructions on her computer called "code" that told robots what to do. These are some of her amazing robot creations.

The Brocc Bot
could hide broccoli.

The Blotter Bot
could finger paint.

Mischief Bot did the opposite
of what you told her to do.

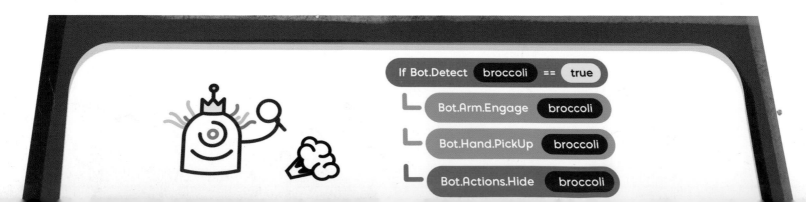

If Bot.Detect broccoli == true

Bot.Arm.Engage broccoli

Bot.Hand.PickUp broccoli

Bot.Actions.Hide broccoli

"CLEAN! THIS! MESS!
Or I'm taking away your computer."

Uh-oh. Dad
wasn't impressed.

Rox fumed.

"Pack up the dollhouse?"

"Hang up the hula hoops?"

"Organize the race cars?"

More chores meant less time to play!

"Hmmmm," Rox thought. "Dad wants to take away my computer.

But what if I use it to make a robot to do my chores for me?"

YES!

Rox laid out her colored pencils and drafting paper and started thinking.
What would her robot need to do?

1. Identify a mess

2. Organize it

3. Find another mess

CHOREBOT

Her robot would need:

BATTERIES

(his heart)

A CIRCUIT BOARD

(his brains)

SCRAPS OF METAL

(his skin)

HELLO

A SPEECH SYNTHESIZER

(his voice)

PIPES AND WIRES

(to connect it all together)

A NINJA HEADBAND

(just 'cause)

Rox welded all the parts together and wrote line after line of code that instructed her robot to sort unorganized objects by color and type.

Now all her creation needed was a little more superpower.

The most powerful technology in the world is "artificial intelligence." This code gives robots the power to learn on their own without humans telling them what to do.

If her robot had it, Rox wouldn't have to update him every time she made a new kind of mess.

There was just one problem. According to legend, robots with artificial intelligence could become so smart that they might rebel against their bosses.

This was a risk Rox was willing to take. It would be her super secret.

```
While Chorebot.Detect  thing  ==  true
    Organize  thing  by  color  type
    if Chorebot.Detect  thing  !=  true
        thing = new Chorebot.execute  SecretCode, AI
```

Rox pressed 'Enter' and, in a cloud of lightning and popcorn, Chorebot thundered to life!

IT'S ALIVE!

Rox twisted the dial and Chorebot zoomed off.

He packed up the dollhouse, hung up the hula hoops,
and organized the race cars.

Before Rox could make another mess, her robot zipped into the next room.

He rearranged the closets by color and pattern.

He coordinated the books by width and height.

At first, mom and dad were skeptical. But once Chorebot cleaned up their messes, they came around and raised a juice box. "Cheers to that!"

MESS. MUST ORGANIZE.

Searching for another mess, Chorebot's circuits began to tingle.

The yard next door was an unkempt catastrophe!

Chorebot scurried across the lawn.

He hemmed the hedges, lined up the lilies, and trimmed the tulips.

HAPPY?

Rox stumbled outside in disbelief. Her robot was learning...and growing!

Before she could explain to her neighbor Amar

what was happening, Chorebot raced up the street.

He skidded to a halt. So many poorly parked cars and untidy trees!
He started cleaning it all up.

Rox and Amar stared at the spruced-up street.

"He's still learning! And growing even more!" Rox cried.

Chorebot found his next target: downtown. What a disorganized, dilapidated, disastrous dilemma! He piled up houses, interlocked glass towers, and stacked concrete buildings.

MESS!

People started to panic. Mr. Abdullah couldn't find his apartment.

Mrs. Zhang didn't want to live at the top of a stack!

Everyone running around in circles caught Chorebot's eye.

People! With their colorful clothing, peculiar personalities, and mismatched moods. What a mess!

He divided everyone up by type and style. He separated boys from girls,

blues from pinks, shorts from skirts, business from casual.

The colorful patterns thrilled Chorebot out of his artificial mind!

Enough was enough. Rox wanted her robot to put toys in bins and clothing in drawers...not people in boxes!
Rox knew what she had to do: CLEAN. THIS. MESS.

Uh oh.

"Amar, I can't find a solution without the internet!" Rox panicked. "And now the city is doomed."

"The internet didn't make Chorebot." Amar encouraged his friend.

"You did, Rox. And you can fix him!"

Rox wiped her tears and got to work. "How can I make Chorebot undo everything?" she thought.

"I know! That's what my Mischief Bot does...the opposite of what she's told to do! If Chorebot had her code, he'd put everything back!"

Rox updated the code and turned to Amar. "Here, wear my tutu."

Amar raised an eyebrow. Rox explained her master plan. "With this outfit, Chorebot won't know which box to put you in. While he's distracted, I'll install the new code."

Amar squeezed into the tutu. The bait was set.

It was time for Rox to work her magic.

Chorebot scooped up Amar and analyzed him.
Did he go with the boy batch, the girl group,
the skirt pile, or the hat pack?

CAN. NOT. COM. PUTE.

The robot was stumped.
Amar didn't fit in a box!

Hiya! Rox jammed in the new code and Chorebot froze.

His eyes started spinning like two giant beach balls.

Was he debugged...or about to bug out?

Chorebot roared back to life. SCHWOOP! He dispersed the buildings. VROOM! He reparked the cars. WHOOSH! He smoothed the sidewalks. Everyone high-fived. Their old city was back!

"Fist-bump for the raddest girl in town!"

"Uh, can I have my tutu back?"

"Actually, I like the way it breathes."

Back at home, Rox burst through the door.

"Dad! Chorebot almost destroyed the city, and then I TOTALLY
SAVED THE DAY!" Dad turned a page, enjoying a book from their
color-coordinated library. "That's great, honey."

"Boss Rox?" Chorebot looked rather frazzled.

"I'm confused. My goal was to organize, yet after I worked so hard for you, you still weren't happy. I think I'm burnt-out."

BURNT-OUT

"No, you did great!
But I gave you the wrong direction.
Why don't you take some time off and
figure out what you love doing most!"

A few days later, Chorebot was happily hemming the hedges, lining up the lilies, and trimming the tulips, when he realized what he was meant to be...a Gardenbot!

As for Rox, it was time to take a break from her coding superpowers.

She'd get started on her next project tomorrow.

This story is over, but the next one is about to begin.

CODE A ROBOT IN YOUR LIVING ROOM!

⚡ Download the Secret Code app.

⚡ Transform the book cover into a coding game.

⚡ Create your own robot in augmented reality!

GET STARTED NOW!

YOURSECRETCODE.COM/GAME

MIA'S PANCAKE BOT

{CREATED BY} ⓘ MARA.LECOCQ

MARA LECOCQ

Mara grew up on a steady diet of technology, painting, and feminism. After spending her childhood in the Philippines coding and designing websites, Mara later built a successful career in New York as a creative director, launching tech products and campaigns for the world's biggest brands. As one of the rare female leaders, Mara decided to do something about the lack of diversity in technology by encouraging girls' aspirations in their formative years.

With Rox's Secret Code and its universe, Mara is on a mission to plant seeds that can grow into fulfilling futures.

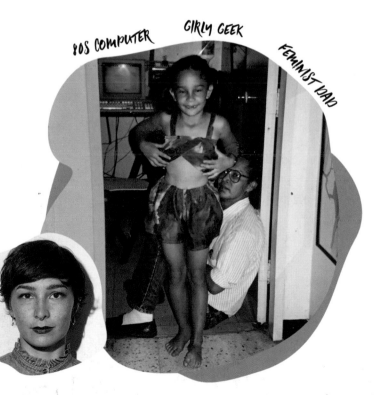

80S COMPUTER GIRLY GEEK FEMINIST DAD

{WRITTEN BY} ⓘ NKARCH

NATHAN ARCHAMBAULT

Nathan is a creative director and author who splits his time between making ads, writing books, and inspiring his two young daughters, Winter and Aurora, to discover their own superpowers.

{ILLUSTRATED BY} ⓘ JESSVONI

JESSIKA VON INNEREBNER

Jess loves illustrating stories of super-sheroes, skater rockstars, and baseball princesses. In spare moments, she can be found dancing, long-boarding, traveling to distant lands, chasing adventure, and laughing with friends.

{TECH LED BY} ⓘ PLATYPUSSDIVVA

RODOLFO DENGO

Rodolfo is passionate about intersectional feminism, and is the proud father of a feisty little girl, Emma. Tinkering with all things mechanical and digital, he codes and leads technology for Secret Code's customizable products.

ROX'S SECRET CODE

Text © 2018 by Mara Lecocq and Nathan Archambault.
Illustrations © 2018 by Jessika Von Innerebner
Tech © 2018 led by Rodolfo Dengo.
Coding game by Electric Factory.
www.yoursecretcode.com

Published by POW!
A division of powerHouse
Packaging & Supply, Inc. 32 Adams Street, Brooklyn, NY 11201-1021 · info@powkidsbooks.com ·
www.powkidsbooks.com · www.powerHouseBooks.com · www.powerHousePackaging.com ·

Printed by Asia Pacific Offset
Library of Congress Control Number: 2018948139
ISBN: 978-1-57687-899-6 · 10 9 8 7 6 5 4 3 2 1
Printed in China